In Loving Memory

Julia B. Mosher

OLD HIPPO'S EASTER EGG

BY JAN WAHL

Illustrations by Lorinda Bryan Cauley

NEW YORK   HARCOURT BRACE JOVANOVICH   LONDON

JE

Requests for permission to make copies of
any part of the work should be mailed to:
Permissions, Harcourt Brace Jovanovich, Inc.,
757 Third Avenue, New York, New York 10017

Printed in the United States of America

LIBRARY OF CONGRESS CATALOGING IN PUBLICATION DATA
Wahl, Jan.
Old Hippo's easter egg.
SUMMARY: Old Hippo receives an Easter egg out of
which hatches a duckling—the son he's always wanted.
[1. Animals—Fiction. 2. Friendship—Fiction.
3. Easter stories] I. Cauley, Lorinda Bryan.
II. Title.
PZ7.W1266Ol   [E]   79–9199
ISBN 0–15–257835–8
ISBN 0–15–668452–7 pbk.

First edition
B C D E

June '82   Gift

To
PAT
fondly

and to
Plum and Bliss

Old Hippo sat on his front porch
watching rain drizzle.
The moon was lying in the clouds,
and colors of tulips glowed across
the soft night.

"Tomorrow is Easter!" he grumped.
"I will be alone as usual.
   If I only had a child to paint eggs for."

"What about ME?" asked a tiny voice.
   It was Pocket Mouse, who lived
   in Old Hippo's vest pocket.

"You're too old to be a child."
 Old Hippo sighed. "You're old like me.
 And *alone.*"
"Except for you," said Pocket Mouse,
 snuggling down.

The wind shook the porch. The two went
inside where it was cozy.
Outside a figure in a shawl splashed
in the wet. It set a basket at the door
and slunk off.

Old Hippo and Pocket Mouse ate dinner
and went to bed.

Easter morn was silver shiny.
Old Hippo found the basket, which was
tied with sky blue ribbon.
"Good!" He laughed. "I love a
hard-boiled egg."
He took it in his paw and
lifted his spoon to crack it.

"WAIT!" cried Pocket Mouse.
"Don't you hear a noise?"
Old Hippo put the egg against his ear.

"You are right. Something is
   moving in there," said Old Hippo.
He lit a candle and peered at the egg.
Something wiggled.

"It must be hatched!
   One of us must sit on it," said Old Hippo.
He paused.
"I am too big," he admitted.
"And I am too small," said Pocket Mouse.

Now they heard a noise outside.
The Easter Parade!
A tuba boomed, *"Oom pah pah."*
Mole, Badger, Bear, and
Rooster came marching, showing
off brand-new clothes.

None of them seemed right as a hatcher.
At the end of the line came
Auntie Sheep.
Pocket Mouse squeaked,
"She is perfect!"
and Old Hippo ran to beg her.

"Don't know much about egg-hatching,"
said Auntie. "But I can try."
She smiled, chose a comfortable chair,
and sat quiet as cotton wool.
Old Hippo brought her tea.

While she sat hatching,
he cooked for her
the choicest of meals.
Pocket Mouse did entertaining tricks.

One morning, early, Auntie Sheep
gave a shriek and jumped up.
"Crick! Crack!" Out rolled a yellow ball.
Hippo and Mouse and Auntie
stared with amazement.

"Is it a boy or girl?"
asked Old Hippo eagerly.
Bright eyes blinked and gazed up at him.
It had a big bill and feet and
tumbled and walked just
like a wind-up toy.

It followed Old Hippo everywhere.
"Mama!" it called him.
"I will call my new son Small Quack!"
sang Old Hippo, beaming.

Auntie Sheep went home to her meadow.

One day Pocket Mouse
and Old Hippo took Small Quack waddling.
A grasshopper, a beetle, and
a hundred-legger scared him.
But after a bit he chased them.

As they sat by the pond,
a crow passed above, and
Small Quack asked:
"Will *I* fly like that?"

Old Hippo frowned. "Bosh! Who wants to fly?
Spend your time in the lovely water
and wallow in the mud!
I did it when I was young," he said.
In a boat Pocket Mouse and he sat
teaching Small Quack how to swim.

A bright white butterfly flashed
in the sky, and Small Quack's
big eyes opened wide.
"Watch me. I am a butterfly!" he shouted,
flapping with his wings.

Wobbling, the duck rose into the air.
Higher. Higher.
"Come back! I was going
to bake cookies!" cried Old Hippo.
Small Quack fluttered down.

Autumn blew in, crisp and chilly.
Pocket Mouse taught Small Quack ABC's
while Old Hippo baked.

One morning before everyone arose,
Wild Goose poked her head
in the window. "Better get moving,
boy. Don't stick around!"
she called. Then she flew south.

All at once Small Quack
blinked both eyes and shook his
wings. He knew it was true.
He was *born* to *fly*—
TO FLY WHERE HE MUST!

So on a brown falling-leaf day,
with help from the wind, Small Quack
flew up, up and over the horizon.

Pocket Mouse and Old Hippo wept
and waved.
"Good-bye! Good-bye!"

Old Hippo poured hot tea for
Pocket Mouse and moaned in a low,
cracked voice:
"Always wished for a son.
   And now he is GONE." He sighed.
"Well, I have you."

"Yes! But it's time
   for my long winter nap,"
   said Pocket Mouse, yawning.
   He put food in his mouth
   and dug a tunnel under the rug.
   The winter sky turned to gray
   and snow twinkled down.
   Old Hippo's vest pocket was empty,
   and so was his heart.

"Why must I spend each winter
   ALONE?" he asked in
   the hall of the silent house.

On Christmas Eve Old Hippo stared
at the fire, thinking
he saw Small Quack flying
over the sparks. The clock struck ten.
Up he went to bed.
He dreamed over and over again
that friends knocked below,
eager to come in.

At last one spring morning
came a real knock at the door.
It was Pocket Mouse.
He had dug a tunnel in his sleep
out into the yard
when he heard seeds and buds growing.

"Guess who?" he said.
"And guess who I found on the
front step?"

"Small Quack, my son!" cried
   Old Hippo. "You've come home."

"I can't stay," said Small Quack.
"I got married. Now I am Big Quack.
   And you are a grandfather!"

He placed a box tied with grass
green ribbon in Old Hippo's hands.

Then he flew slowly into the sky.

Gently Old Hippo opened the box.
It was an egg—a new child to hatch.

"Do you think it will stay?"
asked Old Hippo, smiling.

Pocket Mouse stayed silent.

"Never mind," Old Hippo said.
"I will love it anyway.
    Go and find Auntie Sheep."